I0734512

MARY CRAWFORD

THE Price OF Freedom

HIDDEN BEAUTY NOVELLA 2

COPYRIGHT

Hidden Beauty Series

Until the Stars Fall from the Sky
So the Heart Can Dance
Joy and Tiers
Love Naturally
Love Seasoned
Love Claimed
If You Knew Me (and other silent musings) (novella)
Jude's Song
The Price of Freedom (novella)
Paths Not Taken
Dreams Change (novella)
Heart Wish (100% charity release)
Tempting Fate
The Letter
The Power of Will

Hidden Hearts Series

Identity of the Heart
Sheltered Hearts
Hearts of Jade
Port in the Storm (novella)
Love is More Than Skin Deep
Tough
Rectify
Pieces (a crossover novel)
Hearts Set Free
Freedom (a crossover novel)
The Long Road to Love (novella)
Love and Injustice (Protection Unit)
Out of Thin Air (Protection Unit)
Soul Scars (Protection Unit)

OTHER WORKS:
The Power of Dictation
Use Your Voice
Vision of the Heart
An Everyday Guide to Scrivener 3 for Mac
Vision of the Heart#AmWriting: A Collection of
Letters to Benefit The Wayne Foundation

DEDICATION

For military families

facing tough choices

Thank you for your service.

CHAPTER ONE

NATE

MY MOM SHOVES THE forms back across the table at me. "No! I'm not looking at these."

"But Mom —"

"No 'but Mom' here. What are you trying to do, break my heart?"

I sigh. I knew this was going to be hard, but I never wanted this decision to hurt my mom. Tracy Abernethy has had more than her fair share of heartbreak.

"I'm simply trying to honor Dad."

"Nathaniel, if you want to do that just do some volunteer work for a veterans charity or something. You don't have to go sign up to be a soldier. You know what the Army did to your father. Why would you trust them to treat you any better?" My mom slumps against the back of the booth. She looks shattered.

"Dad was blown up by insurgents, Mom. It wasn't the Army who killed him."

"What difference does it make in your life? Your dad was still dead, and I was still a single mom. Why would I want to give them another person I love?" My mom grabs a napkin from the dispenser and wipes her eyes. The other diners are giving us curious looks and several are scowling at me.

"Mom, please try to understand." I run a hand through my brown hair. "I'm Nathaniel Andrew Abernathy the Third. Our family has served honorably in the military for three generations. It's my turn to step up and finish what Dad started."

"Your dad wouldn't want me to send you off to be sacrificed — especially since you're all I have left."

"You don't know! Dad was so proud of his military service and the fact that he followed in his father's footsteps. Why wouldn't he want me to do the same?"

"Your father was blown to bits trying to serve his country," my mom screams at me with tears in her eyes.

Everyone in the restaurant stops what they're doing to look at us. What used to be a comfortably loud mom-and-pop restaurant is now deadly silent as everyone watches the drama unfold in front of them.

"Mom, I know." I say in a low voice. "Why do you think I want to stop these terrorists? I don't want any other kids to go through what I went through. I don't want the terrorists to win and create any more single moms and lonely widows."

My mom leans forward and stirs her coffee in short, jerky strokes. The stress lines on her face are looking more pronounced by the moment. "What about college? You're halfway through your junior year. What happens to your scholarship? Are you throwing it all away?"

"No … well … I guess maybe, yes. But, I should be able to get help through the Army when I'm done," I stammer as I shrug.

My mom's face is grim. "What about your language program? What happens if you just drop out? You worked so hard to get where you are — why throw it all away?"

"I know, I thought about those things. Serving overseas would help my Arabic." I sigh. I guess I should have prepared more thoroughly for this conversation. I didn't even think of any counter arguments in advance. I guess I expected a different reaction from my mom. When I was growing up, she seemed supportive of all things military.

"Why couldn't you take Spanish or French? Even German? Why Arabic?" Her curls become more haphazard as she rakes her fingers through her hair.

"Dad was one of the best translators out there. I don't want to shame his memory. I want to be as good as he was."

"You know, I used to be proud that you taught yourself Arabic. Now I wish you'd rather goofed off and played with video games and skateboards."

"This isn't a random, spur-of-the-moment decision. I've been working toward this goal for as long as I can remember."

"What did your advisor at school say? This is a big decision for you to make by yourself."

"Geez Mom, I'm almost twenty-one."

"When you have some perspective, you'll understand that twenty-one is impossibly young."

"Dad was nineteen when he joined." I argue as I remember meeting my dad at the airport every time he returned from a deployment. I thought he was tougher than any super hero.

"Yeah, he was — and a decade later, he was dead. Is that what you want for your life?"

"Tyler and Trevor say the odds of me being killed are slim, especially with the MOS I'd like to pursue."

"You're talking to Tyler Colton?" My mom's eyes go wide. "You do realize he was in charge of the mission which killed your dad, don't you? Why would you take his advice about anything?"

"Tyler's a great guy. He still feels bad about Dad. He's told me more than once that he'd go back and change it if he could. Dad wasn't the only person screwed up by the incident. Trevor lost his leg. Tyler still suffers from post-traumatic stress disorder with the brain injury he got. No one got off scot-free."

"Knowing all he knows about the risks, you're telling me Tyler is suggesting that you join the military? I would think he would want to steer clear of it as much as possible."

"Tyler's not anti-military; he simply wants more safety protocols put in place to prevent the type of incident that killed Dad and required Tyler and Trevor to get medical discharges."

"What's to say they've done anything about the safety risks? Are the vehicles and flack vests more fortified now? Do they have foolproof intel?"

"Mom! They'll never make war one hundred percent safe —"

"I just don't see why you can't honor your dad's legacy somewhere else like an embassy somewhere. What about the State Department? That's safe."

"Were you proud of Dad when you guys first got married — when he was a soldier? Forget about what happened later. In the beginning … did you support him?"

"I did. I'll always remember. That's what makes me so scared for you. Nathaniel, you're still a baby. You don't know what's dangerous yet."

"Mom, I'm not going into this blind. I've already taken the ASVAB. I've been working out and increasing my endurance so I can do well in basic. I have my bases covered, Mom."

"Except you've forgotten something really important."

"What?" I suck down the milkshake melting in front of me.

"Not what — who."

"Holly?" I ask, my voice growing louder. "I haven't forgotten about her. I could never forget her."

"Well, it sure seems like it."

"I've been in love with her since the seventh grade." I lean closer, dropping my voice. "This isn't a perfect plan, mom, but we all have to make sacrifices for it to work. Everyone in the military does. Why should I be any different?"

"I know Holly doesn't want to make a big deal out of this. She certainly doesn't want us to treat her any differently, but this is different. Very different."

"You think I don't know Holly is living on borrowed time?" I snap, shoving my glass aside with the back of my hand. "I know that with every beat of my heart."

"Then why do you want to leave her?"

"Because sometimes you're forced to decide between two rights and someone always pays a price."

"What does Holly say about all this? I can't imagine she's happy." My mom crosses her arms and sits back in her chair.

"I don't know." I look away. "I haven't told her yet. I wanted to come to you first."

"For Pete's sake, Nathaniel," my mom exclaims as her eyes tear up again. "Did you think I'd be throwing you a ticker-tape parade for putting yourself in the line of fire?"

"I thought you would be proud of me."

"I am proud of you." My mom leans across the table and grabs hold of my hand. "Your father would probably be busting his buttons with pride. But, I don't know if you're doing the right thing."

"I get it, Mom, I really do. But it's time for me to fulfill my legacy."

Chapter Two

Holly

I'M EXHAUSTED. DESPITE SEVERAL nebulizer treatments, I still can't catch my breath. I think I might have to go back to the doctor and change up my antibiotics, which sucks. I'm in the middle of dead week and my classes are a pain this term.

I make myself some tea and cuddle in my favorite blanket on the couch. I put a random documentary on TV and try to watch, but my eyes are too heavy.

My eyes pop open when my stomach growls. As I shake off the fog from my unscheduled nap, my nose twitches at the smell of rich tomato sauce. That can only mean one thing.

"Nate?"

He peeks around the corner holding a loaf of French bread. "Afternoon, my Sleeping Beauty. Rough day?"

I start to cough violently, and it seems like forever until I can catch my breath. Nate walks over to my bookshelf, grabs a rescue inhaler, and hands it to me. Then he expertly sets up my breathing treatment in the nebulizer.

"Do you need to put on your vest? I still need to cook the noodles, so it'll be a bit before dinner is ready."

"No, I just had a percussive treatment. Unfortunately, I think I'm getting sick."

Nick's mouth tightens and his shoulders droop. "I thought your new antibiotics were supposed to stop any new crud."

"You know how it goes." I shrug. "I have no immune system left. This could be viral for all I know. Whatever it is, I feel like crap."

"I'm sorry Hol. I wish I could make it better." Nate's voice is tight, his face pinched.

"I know you do." I look at his clothes and his mussed-up hair. "What are you doing here? I thought you had to work today."

"The new manager double-booked the shift, so I came home to give you a study break."

The words seem innocent, but there's something off about Nate's body language. As I study Nate closer, I notice he seems exhausted too. His affable smile is missing, and he looks nervous. Before I say anything else, I break out into another round of coughing which makes me feel like my ribs are cracking underneath the pressure.

"Sit back and do your treatment," Nate says, pressing me back into the couch.

"Dinner will be ready in a few."

⬤•⬤

Nate is barely looking at me and saying even less. I don't know what's going on; Nate and I have known each other since we were eleven years old. We can usually finish each other's sentences.

"Nate, this was incredibly delicious and sweet of you to make. Can you please just tell me what's really going on? This weirdness is freaking me out."

"I wanted to talk to you." Nate sighs. "But you don't feel well, so I'll do it later."

"Newsflash: I have cystic fibrosis. Technically, I won't ever feel one hundred percent. You might as well tell me what's going on."

"Are you sure? I can wait until you're a little stronger —" he asks pensively.

"Come on, Nate. You know tomorrow could be worse than today."

"I get it. Still, I don't want to be responsible for causing a setback."

"Nathaniel Abernethy, you promised never to treat me with kid gloves," I challenge, placing my hands on my hips. "You're the one person I don't have to hide from. You know what my life is like and love me anyway, so stop treating me like I'm going to break."

"I do love you, that's what makes this difficult."

"Nate, you're scaring me. What's going on?" I ask insistently. Usually, Nate is blunt and upfront. His sudden reticence to talk is disconcerting.

Nate crumples up the paper towel in his lap as he says, "I don't even know where to start."

"Just pick a place."

"Do you know how excruciating it is to choose between the two things I love."

"Wait — are you breaking up with me?" My heart beats a million miles an hour. "What did I do?"

"Nothing —"

"This is about the CF, isn't it? It's too much. I knew it! Well, screw you!" I throw my napkin on the table and storm to my bedroom.

Even though I want to try to pretend this isn't devastating, it totally is. I thought Nate would always be in my corner. What happened? Things were going so well. Angry tears stream down my face. Who was I fooling, thinking I could have a normal life with a husband? My fate was sealed the moment I was conceived. The crazy thing is I have a brother and sister, and they are fine. Most days I am absolutely thrilled they're okay, but some days — like today — it pisses me off that I was the unlucky one.

I try to stop the sobs from coming — crying won't make my mucus situation any better — and bury my head under my pillow as I try to compose myself. Nate does not need to know how much he's devastated me. I don't want to give him that power. I thought my day was hard before, but this is exponentially harder.

There's a soft knock on my door.

"Go away!" I wheeze.

"Holly, I need to talk to you."

"I don't want to hear anything you want tell me. I swear you don't want to hear what I have to say to you." I try to catch my breath.

"Don't be like this —"

I can hear him shuffling around on the other side of my door. I can almost see him slouching as he stuffs his hands in his pockets.

"I'm tired, Nate, so just go. Maybe tomorrow will be better."

Nate growls in frustration. "If that's what you want, I'll go. But I'm coming back tomorrow because I have something to say."

"Right now the jury is still out about whether I'll be calm enough to listen."

"Holly, I love you. Don't forget."

"Doesn't feel like it," I accuse. It's too late. He's already gone and I break down into another round of tears.

CHAPTER THREE

NATE

SITTING BEHIND THE WHEEL of my car, I smack my steering wheel so hard it makes my hand sting. I can't believe how quickly our conversation got derailed. Regardless of what Holly thinks, I'm not planning to ditch her. This was never about her cystic fibrosis.

I know I shouldn't be surprised. Holly has a fiery temper. She's always been one to take action first and ask questions later. That's how we met in the sixth grade; I was sitting at the edge of the playground wallowing in my grief about my dad when a ball came hurtling in my direction. I caught it and threw it back to the guys playing dodgeball. Except, it wasn't their ball. The next thing I knew this little sprite of a girl was chewing me up one side and down the other for stealing her ball. It took me four more recesses to convince her I didn't steal it on purpose.

Despite our rocky start, we've been best friends since that year. She was there for me in a way few others, including my mother, were. She seemed to understand my sense of loss about my dad. Around her, I didn't need to be rough, tough, and manly. I could simply be Nate. Honestly, I don't know what I'd do without her — and I don't want to figure that out now.

Placing my dad's favorite Toby Keith CD in the deck, I turn my music on in my truck and back out of her driveway. I try to figure out a way to regroup on the drive home.

All I know is that I love Holly and I won't let her go without a fight.

• • •

I've spoken with Tyler Colton over the phone several times, but I've never met him in person. However, I figure this conversation needs to be done face-to-face. It took a two-hour drive to get here.

Now that I'm face-to-face with him, I'm not sure what I plan to say.

I study the imposing man with wavy hair and try to imagine him being one of my father's best friends. Although he is somber and buttoned up in his Sheriff's uniform at the moment, there are pictures all over his office of him wearing a cowboy hat and laughing with his wife. My mom always told me my father had a wicked sense of humor. As I glance at the pictures, I can understand why they were good friends.

Tyler does a comical double take when I take my hat off and take a seat opposite Tyler. "You probably get this all the time, but you look just like your dad, Abernathy. It's like seeing a ghost." Tyler says as he sits down in the booth. "I was a little worried I wouldn't be able to pick you out of the crowd, but it was no problem."

I chuckle awkwardly. "It's all right — I hear it all the

time. I look so much like him that I think it's hard for my mom. My grandmother has Alzheimer's, and she actually believes I am my dad."

"That must be hard all around. I'm sorry." Tyler shakes his head. "You'll never know how I wish I could turn back time and make different choices."

I lean forward in my chair as I hold my hat in my hands. I look him directly in the eyes. "Officer Colton, I didn't come here to make you feel bad about what happened. I understand terrorists were to blame for my dad's death. You can't take that on yourself."

"I was his commanding officer, Abernathy. It was my responsibility to keep him safe. There was something in the logistics that we just didn't know."

"They're called terrorists because they strike at random," I can't stand to look in his guilt-ridden eyes a second longer. They remind me too much of my mom's. I stand and pace in a regimented line in front of a bookcase. "My dad knew the cost of war; he used to speak to me about what I would need to do if he didn't come back every time he set out — how I'd have to be the man of the house, to take care of my mom. He knew the risks."

"It's our responsibility to make life for our soldiers as safe as possible — even in the middle of a war zone. That day, things went terribly wrong."

"We can't go back and change things. They are what they are," I declare philosophically.

"True enough." Tyler picks up a small picture of his wife and holds it like a talisman. "If we're looking toward the future, what can I do for you?"

Suddenly unnerved, I shove an envelope to Tyler. "I

need your advice. I thought I had made a good plan, but everyone I know seems upset by my choice. Don't they understand I'm almost twenty-one and it is my choice?"

"What did you expect? Your dad was killed in action. Army can't be the most popular choice of possible occupations under those circumstances. If you were my son, I'd probably try to talk you out of it and steer you to something safer."

"It was good enough for my dad and my grandfather, why isn't it good enough for me?"

"Because your family has seen the ugly side of war. They don't want to put you at risk," Tyler answers before he takes a sip of his coffee.

"But you went back after you were injured and you know first-hand the horrors of what happened."

Tyler sighs. "Yes, I went back — but it was one of the hardest things I've ever had to do. If it wasn't for the love of my wife, I don't know if I would have ever made it through. Even so, it took an emotional toll on me and my marriage."

"So why do you continue to do it? You could retire. You definitely have enough time in."

"I ask myself that question every time I have to pack up and ship out. For me, it's because I left a job undone. I needed to find the people who killed your dad and injured the rest of my squad. The terrorists needed to pay for their actions."

"So how is what you did any different from what I want to do?"

"It isn't — but you're so young. You have so much going for you. A full scholarship ride on academic merit? It's not everyone who gets such a great opportunity."

"Still, I made a promise to my dad that if something ever happened to him, I'd take over where he left off. In my mind, that means finishing what he started even if it means waiting to go to college."

"I made the same decision. Thought the same thing," he says, pointing to his high school diploma sitting on a shelf above his head. "I never finished my degree. Army life kept getting in the way. It's likely one reason your mom can't accept your choice."

"She's scared I won't make it home, like Dad. But how do I convince her I will? I'm just going over to be a translator. It's not like I'll be doing hand-to-hand combat on the front lines."

"It's not so simple, Abernathy." Tyler scrubs his hand down his face as if he's trying to wipe out some invisible vision. "War is dangerous regardless of what field you're in."

"I guess that's why my dad used to tell her he was being careful. Maybe that's why she went ballistic when I said something similar. I don't know what to do, Colonel. My mom has always been my biggest supporter. I worry about leaving her alone because it's pretty much been the two of us."

"Are you willing to go against everyone in your family to serve your country? I have to tell you, I'm not sure if it's the right strategy. To be a successful soldier, you need to know there are people at home in your corner. Otherwise, it can be terribly isolating."

"My mom will come around eventually. I guess I caught her off guard with my announcement; she was looking forward to my graduation from college."

"That's understandable. What does your girlfriend

say?"

"Don't get me started. That conversation was the biggest SNAFU ever. I didn't even get a chance to share my news; she thinks I'm breaking up with her."

"Signing up for the military is a big deal. It's not like you can change your mind after a couple of months. You need to make sure you're doing what's right for you."

"How do I know I'm making the right choice when I have so many people who count on me?"

"There are no easy answers. The military has many great things to offer, but you have to balance that against the reality of your life."

"I don't even want to think about the nuts and bolts."

"Why not?" Tyler's brow creases with concern.

"Because if I'm forced to look at the reality of my life, it's pretty dismal. The woman I love will die soon, and there isn't anything I can do about it."

"We're all going to lose our partners; it's simply a matter of time. No one is immune."

"You don't understand, sir. This is not merely a philosophical discussion for me; Holly will actually die — probably before her fortieth birthday. She's only twenty-one, but she still has giant struggles every day."

"That's too bad, Nate. I guess you have a lot more to factor into your decision."

"I know — except Holly's always wanted me to treat her no differently than anyone else."

"The stubborn ones always keep you on your toes." Tyler smirks. "I've got one of my own and I can't imagine my life without her."

Chapter Four

Holly

I'VE BEEN TRYING TO ignore Nate, but he's making it impossible. Every half hour he sends me a gif or a tweet to remind me that he loves me. It's weird because I was convinced he was all set to break up with me. I don't know how much longer I can hold out.

The professor nails me with a stare. "Ms. Caldwell do you need me to repeat the assignment? It doesn't look like you've been very attentive."

I realize I've blanked out everything in my Creative Writing class. I can't remember anything the professor said because I'm so focused on trying to sort out what Nate is doing.

I snap to attention. "I'm sorry, Professor Wallace. I have a personal crisis."

"Deal with it on your own time, Ms. Caldwell."

"Yes, sir."

As I leave the classroom, Nate is standing by the door waiting for me.

"What are you doing here? I have a class in like eight

minutes."

"No, you don't. It's been canceled; there is a sign on the door. Let's go have some coffee. The place on the corner is dead this time of day." Nate offers.

We walk in silence to the coffee shop. After, we find a dark little cove in the back corner, I demand, "What do you want from me?"

"I'm not breaking up with you, Holly. I love you."

"I know you do. Sometimes I wonder if it's fair that you fell in love with me."

"If love was fair, my mom wouldn't have been left alone, and my grandma would remember who my grandpa is."

"Still —"

"I didn't choose to fall in love with you, Holly. It's part of who I am; I can't remember a time when I wasn't. I don't know if fate, God, or anyone else cares about how fair it is. It just is."

"I don't want to live scared, but right now, I'm so scared I can barely stand. I don't know what my cystic fibrosis means for our future, for us."

My heart beats a little harder. The grim set of Nate's jaw tells me this will be a very difficult conversation to have.

Nate orders our favorite coffees and smiles at the barista. She blushes deeply before practically skipping off. I don't blame her—a smile from my handsome boyfriend still makes my knees weak. My stomach drops to my toes when Nate gets up to dig out my rescue inhaler from my backpack and sets it on the table. *Crap! He thinks whatever he's planning to tell me will cause me to have a coughing attack.*

This does not look good for me.

After the barista brings us our order, Nate takes a long drink of his. "This conversation has nothing to do with your cystic fibrosis."

"Nothing? I find that hard to believe; my CF effects everything."

Nate sits back in his chair. "Okay … I wasn't quite honest. This is about your cystic fibrosis. At least, the decision I have to make will be impacted by your CF. I can't get around our reality."

"Geez, sorry to be such a pain," I retort as I pull away from him.

"If I was bothered by your CF, I would've been gone a long time ago," he answers as he leans toward me.

I sigh and take a drink of my coffee. I try to take a deep breath, but my lungs are feeling gunky today. "This guessing game sucks. Why don't you come out and tell me what you have to say?"

Nate gives me a pained smile. "I don't know if you've noticed, but I've been trying to do that for several days."

I lean forward and put my elbows on the table. "By all means, enlighten me."

"I think it's time," he answers as if I'm supposed to understand what the heck is going on by his simple statement.

"Time for what?" I demand in an exasperated tone.

"To do what I've been preparing to do for as long as I can remember."

All the blood drains from my face.

"I thought when you didn't join the Army right out

of high school, you had changed your mind. I mean, you started college with me and everything."

"No, I didn't actually change my mind. I just wanted a couple more years of Arabic at the college level before I joined."

"So, this is a done deal? You've already signed the paperwork?"

"Not yet — but, I am pretty sure I know what I want to do." He taps a bundle of papers in his pocket. "I didn't want to make this decision without you. To make matters worse, my mom isn't even excited for me."

I shake my head at him in dismay. "Nate, you are a brilliant guy, but did you really expect your mom to be happy about your choice to go off to enlist when she lost her husband in the middle of a war zone? You're asking a little much, don't you think?"

"I thought she would be proud that I want to carry on my dad's legacy."

"She probably is. Although, I bet she's more scared than she is proud. I can't say I blame her. She knows more than most about the price many soldiers' families pay to keep our nation free."

Nate takes another long drink of his coffee. "So, what do you think?"

"Remember how I said I was scared before? I didn't even know the meaning of the word scared until this moment. The thought of you going away is terrifying. I don't have many years left, and I don't want to spend them away from you."

"I don't want to be separated from you either, but I have to follow my dream."

"I'm not really in a position to tell you what to do with your life; I may not be in it too much longer."

"Holly, don't talk like that. There are advances in medical science every single day. They might come up with something soon."

I reach across the table and grab his hands. "I know we don't talk about this too much — because quite frankly it bums me out — but that doesn't change the facts. So let's face it: I will die, probably within the next few years."

"Holly, you don't know —"

I raise my hand. "I was hospitalized three times last year. The doctors had a difficult time treating my pneumonia the last time I was in the hospital. They said it looked like I was getting resistant to the antibiotics. That does not bode well for a person like me."

"You can't lose hope."

"I'm not losing hope; I'm being realistic. From the moment I was born, cystic fibrosis has never been fair. We've always known the odds were not in my favor. You say my CF affects your decision — now you know the facts."

"There's that stupid word: 'fair'. What if I don't want that to be our ending? What are we going to do?" Nate asks with a haunted expression.

I'm torn. This is one of those situations where what's best for me isn't necessarily the best for us. Nate needs to go on with his life after I'm gone. There's only one thing I can do, even though it breaks my heart.

With difficulty, I take a breath and declare, "I suppose we do what we've been doing every day since we met. We try to squeeze the most out of every day until we don't have any more days left. If that means you have to join the military to be happy, then so be it. I will happily be the partner of a soldier."

CHAPTER FIVE

NATE

FOR SEVERAL DAYS, I toss the concept around in my brain; she'll be the partner of an American soldier. As nice as it sounds, it doesn't sound good enough for me. I want something more permanent — a commitment which will stretch across the globe.

Soon, I can't silence the voice screaming in the back of my head. I find myself sitting at my mother's kitchen table asking another hard question. Hopefully, things will go better this time and she will understand where I'm coming from, but I'm still afraid she'll disapprove of the choice I've made.

Her crochet needles stop moving, and she takes a deep breath. Tears come to her eyes. "So now you're telling me not only are you planning to go off to God knows where to fight a war, but you want to get married?"

"I do," I answer with confidence. "You know there's never been anyone else for me but Holly."

"I know, and that's what worries me. You're too young."

"I may be young, but I know what I'm getting into. I have been by Holly's side for every surgery, hospitalization, and setback she's had since I was eleven. I don't plan to be anywhere else."

"Holly's a nice girl, but it's wrong of her to ask you to make that kind of sacrifice. You deserve to live a whole life with your spouse. I know what it's like to be widowed early and it sucks." My mom's voice is anguished. "Don't marry her just because you feel sorry for her."

"Mom, you don't get it. Holly is not asking me to do anything. I want to do this because I love her and I want to be her husband. We have never built our relationship on pity. Holly would not allow it. You know her. She likes to live her life as normally as she possibly can. She would hate it if I let cystic fibrosis determine our future."

"Answer me this — would you be getting married if you weren't going into the military?"

"The timing might be a little different, but I always planned to get married after I graduated from college."

"Are you sure Holly even wants to get married? She's awfully intent on protecting you from your own bad decisions."

"Mom, we've talked about this. You're right, Holly worries about me. Some days she's all right with the concept that she won't live into old age. Other days, it's really hard for her to picture us together knowing that it won't be a long-term thing."

"So why are you taking the risk if you don't think she'll say yes?"

"Because I cherish her. I can't make any other choice. If she's not in my life, I'm not happy. I would rather be with her for a few years than to be with someone else for a lifetime."

⚊⚊⚫⚊⚊

I run my finger around my collar and try to loosen my tie. Yes, I wore a tie for this. Mr. Caldwell sits on the edge of his recliner chair. "What can I do for you?"

I clear my throat nervously. "Well, sir, you know I've been in love with Holly since before I could shave."

"I'm well aware, son. Lucky for you, my daughter loves you too. Otherwise, it would be awkward."

"I know, sir. I'm incredibly lucky a girl like Holly loves me. She is my whole life."

"I'm glad you feel that way," he says with a smile. "But none of this is newsworthy. So … why are you here?"

"I want to ask you for your permission to marry your daughter."

The large man with a greying beard gives me a confused look. "Okay. Do you mean now … or sometime in the future?"

"I'd like to arrange it as soon as possible."

"Nathaniel!" he thunders as his smile disappears. "What did Joni and I tell the two of you about safe sex? It could be dangerous for Holly to get pregnant. The doctors say it would put additional stress on her lungs. We thought the two of you knew better than to take that kind of risk."

"We do," I stammer.

"Then why are you in such a big hurry to get married?" he demands.

"I won't have forever with Holly, sir. I want to spend

as much time married to her as I can. And I'm getting ready to pursue my career as a military translator; Holly would be better protected as my spouse in the event something happened to me."

"I hope that you're not marrying my daughter so you get more pay —"

"Of course not, sir. I'd always planned to marry your daughter. The military just changes the timing."

"What did Holly say about your plans to join the military?"

"She said she loves me and she's willing to do whatever I need to do to be happy."

"Well, far be it from me to stand between you and happiness. But if you do something to hurt my daughter, you will pay. Do you understand?"

"I will do everything in my power to protect your daughter."

"I believe you, son." Mr. Caldwell sighs. "Even so, you need to understand there are certain things you can't protect her from."

"I know that, sir. In the meantime, we plan to live life big and loud."

Chapter Six

Holly

The week after finals, Nate sends me a mysterious text message. It simply says, 'Date Night — dress fancy'.

It's hard to say what Nate views as fancy. Knowing him, it might be his Oregon Ducks jersey without any holes in it. However, just to be on the safe side, I slide into my favorite dress and heels.

When I answer the door, he kisses me deeply. "Oh, you're wearing makeup." He pulls away from me and wipes his lips. "Do I have any lipstick on me?"

I examine him carefully and announce, "No, you're good. Can you tell me why I have makeup on? Where are we going?"

"It's a surprise. You'll have to wait until we get there," he teases.

"Argh! You know I hate surprises. Can you at least tell me if I'm dressed right?"

He pulls back from me and helps me do a little spin in front of him. "You look perfect. You look so amazing, I'm sure people will wonder why you're with a schmuck like me."

I straighten his tie. "That's not true. I think you're the most handsome guy I know — and you clean up so nicely. You are going to look phenomenal in your dress uniform."

"I hope I don't hate it as much as my dad did. Every time he had to wear his, he would complain long and loud."

"Well, if you don't like it, I'll keep your secret."

"We have to get going or we'll be late." Nate grabs my hand and pulls my purse off the hook by the front door.

"We can't be late on mystery date night," I agree as he drags me out the door.

⸻ • ⸻

As I wait for the waiter to bring me my sparkling cider, I look around in amazement. I can't believe we are actually here; I've never eaten at this restaurant before mostly because it's crazy expensive. Our honors program at school had a banquet here, but we didn't try to get tickets because they were so outrageously overpriced. That night, Nate made a bed in the back of his grandpa's truck and took me up into the mountains. We just watched the stars and talked about our dreams. It was so romantic, I didn't miss the Honors Banquet at all.

This place just oozes opulence and class. I'm surprised when Nate suggests we get dessert. He'll probably need to take out a second mortgage to pay for it. When the waitress brings it out to me, I can't comprehend what I'm looking at. It's some sort of fancy cherry cake with a chocolate dome on the top. I don't know if Nate planned this or if it's coincidence, but cherries are one of my favorite foods. Whenever we go out to eat for milkshakes, I always steal his maraschino cherry off the top of his drink.

I glance over at Nate to thank him for my dessert, and I notice he is wiping sweat from his brow.

"Are you okay?" I ask concerned by his weird demeanor.

"Sure. My nerves are just getting to me a little."

"Yeah, this place is a little intimidating. I'm glad we don't eat here all the time. I keep thinking I'm going to spill something."

"Me too." I try to relax, but Nate is looking at my dessert like he's wondering if he can afford it. "You okay?"

Nate clears his throat and says, "Holly, eat your dessert."

I look at the lovely confection in front of me. "I don't know if I can. It's so gorgeous — I don't want to ruin someone's artwork."

"Please do it for me." Nate whips out his cell phone and takes pictures of my dessert. "Now, I've got it saved for posterity. You will be able to prove to our friends we ate here."

"Very funny. You know none of them will care. They still think Little Caesar's pizza is gourmet food."

Nate smirks. "I can't argue with you. Most of my friends have terrible taste. You are the only exception."

"Why thanks. I have the good taste to choose you. That's something —"

"Holly, I love you more than life itself, but you're driving me crazy. Will you please eat your dessert?"

"Well, I'm so stuffed from dinner, I was thinking about having them wrap it up for me so we can take it with us."

"Trust me you don't want to do that —" Nate says almost desperately.

"Okay, okay I didn't know you felt so strongly about me eating dessert." I take the little dessert spoon and crack open the top of my beautiful sweet sculpture.

I gasp as everything becomes clear. No wonder he was acting so weird. When I look up, Nate is on his knee in front of me. He gently plucks the ring out of the center of my dessert and holds it in front of me.

"Holly Erin Caldwell, I have loved you for as long as I can remember. Will you please marry me and make our love story official?"

For a moment, I lose focus. My thoughts are bouncing around like the ball in a pinball machine. I think back to when I was a small child playing house with my brother and sister. I could never be the married one because they always said I would never get married because I wouldn't live long enough.

If I were to pay attention to the part of myself — the one full of common sense, I would tell Nate to not take the risk on me and to save himself from the hurt.

Yet, as my eyes tear up with joy, I can't bring myself to be logical. This is what I have wanted with Nate since we went to our first dance in the eighth grade.

"Holly? Are you planning to answer me?" Nate asks, still balancing on one knee.

The sound of his deep, sexy voice brings me back to reality. "There are a thousand reasons I should probably say no, and none of them have to do with you. So, I'm going to say yes," I blurt as I hold out my hand for him to put the ring on. There is a smattering of applause and cheers after I say yes, but most people are confused by my odd answer.

The thing about cystic fibrosis is that no one can see how ill I really am. Other than being a little on the small side compared to my brother and sister, I look totally normal — if you look past my crazy cough. So, they don't understand why I gave such a strange response to Nate's question.

Nate stands up and envelops me in a tight hug. "Holly, you make me so happy. I can't wait to start our lives together."

I give him a brief kiss. "I can't believe I'm getting married. My mom will probably have a heart attack. When my older sister got married, they took three years to plan the wedding. I'm guessing you don't want to wait three —"

"No, I got my paperwork back from the Army; and I'm due to check-in for basic training in three months. I want us to be married before I have to leave you."

"Wow, talk about putting it all into perspective. We don't have a lot of time to be happy together before Uncle Sam yanks us apart."

Nate sighs. "You're right, and I don't really know a good way around good old-fashioned reality."

"How about next week when we go on our usual date

we make it with a justice of the peace? I love my mom, but she makes wedding shopping seem like a death-match in the WWE. I don't think I can handle school and that much stress from my family. I would rather marry you in private and be happy."

"If it means we become husband-and-wife sooner, I'm all over your idea." I gulp some of my ice water. "Now to break the news to my parents that their little girl is growing up and is going to be a wife. That'll be tricky."

"Oh, I've already done the hard part. Your dad knows you're getting married because he gave me permission to marry you." Nate responds with a slightly smug look.

"Well, there's some good news for a change. Still, I don't know if they'll be okay with not giving me away."

"Don't worry about it, we'll work something out. We love each other. The rest will fall into place."

I swallow back tears. "It always does. We've faced tougher stuff before."

CHAPTER SEVEN

NATE

IF I THOUGHT MY life was chaotic before I asked Holly to marry me, I've just taken it up a thousand notches. Even if you're having a scaled-back wedding, getting everything organized in a week and a half is the definition of crazy.

As I'm trying to plan our little after-party on my computer, my mom comes in my room.

"I can't believe you'll be married in just a few days. What happened to the little boy whose diapers I changed and whose nose I wiped when you had a cold? You are so grown-up that it scares me. You remind me so much of your father — he always took on more responsibility than everyone around him." My mom straightens my bed. She always cleans when she's nervous.

"I know you think I'm upset by the comparisons, but I'm really not." I walk over and give her a hug. "I would give anything to fill his shoes."

She pulls out of my arms and tears gather in her eyes. "Nathaniel Abernathy, don't say that. I don't want you to have to make the same sacrifices your dad did. Letting you go, and giving you the freedom to go into the Army is one of the hardest things I've ever done. It's like my living nightmare."

"I know Mom. I didn't do it to hurt you. I did it to serve my country and to help figure out who killed Dad."

"I thought you told me Tyler hunted them down the last time he went over to serve in the sandbox."

"The way I understand it, the unit found several members of the gang of insurgents who blew up the convoy, but they didn't get everyone. The ringleader somehow managed to escape."

My mom flinches and frowns. "As proud of you as I am, I still don't understand why you feel the need to put yourself at risk. Your dad sacrificed enough for our family. Our debt is paid."

"I need to do more. I'm going to help the rest of my unit kick some insurgent butt."

"I know you well enough to expect nothing less. I wish it didn't have to be like this."

"I know you do, Mom, but I have to make the right choice for Holly and me. I promise I will be careful."

My mom frowns. "Your dad made me the same promise, and I still had to bring him home in a flag draped box."

I hug my mom again. "I'll do my best to make sure that doesn't happen."

"Nate, don't —"

"Umm … Mom, do you mind if I ask another question?"

"Do we have a space to entertain thirty or forty

people? My small nuptial party has suddenly grown. I want to make sure everyone is able to come, but I'm not sure where we'll put everybody."

"Lucky for you, I'm on the management team at a conference center. I'll find you a place. Does Holly have wedding colors picked out?"

"I don't know. I think she got a wedding gown when she was out with her sister and her mom — but she won't show me what it looks like."

"Don't you know you're not supposed to see?"

"I thought it was only an old-fashioned superstition."

"I think this falls under 'If it ain't broke, don't fix it'."

I laugh. "Holly can be plenty superstitious. I guess I'll just have to wait until next week."

"Of course you will. No boys are allowed to see her dress."

"Mom, does this mean you're excited I'm getting married?" I ask.

"I never disliked Holly, it's just that your circumstances are so impossible. I wish we could make everything work out health-wise. I want the two of you to grow old together."

"I know Mom. As a kid, I prayed every night for Holly to be able to get rid of her CF and live forever. After a while, I simply gave up and decided maybe that's not the way it's supposed to go."

⬤ ● ⬤

Tyler's office is filled with tons of memorabilia of his service and his time as an officer with the Sheriff's Department. As I examine his pictures more closely, I come face-to-face with a picture of my dad. People aren't kidding when they say we look remarkably similar; it's like looking in a mirror. His cheesy grin as he holds up a sign which says, 'I love Tracy and Nate' is like a spear to my side. Sometimes, it's hard to put into words how much I've lost.

Tyler comes into his office and sees me examining the picture. "Oh shoot! If I would've known you were coming today, I would've put those away. That must be difficult for you."

After I wipe away the tears from the corners of my eyes, I gaze up at him. "It's all right. I think it was meant to be. I think this picture shows the only thing I need to know about my dad. I want to be the kind of husband he was."

"Yeah, I got the email. Congratulations."

"Actually, that's why I'm here today. I wanted to know if you would do me a favor?"

"Shoot," Tyler instructs with a smile.

"Well, since I don't have a dad, I wondered if you would come to the ceremony as kind of a stand-in for him."

"I would be honored, but I don't think I'm your mother's favorite person. It might make her profoundly sad or angry to see me. Your mother has more than enough reason to totally hate my guts."

"I already spoke to her; she thinks it would be a good idea for you to be at the wedding. You were the last person to see my dad alive. I think there would be a great deal of positive karma from your presence."

"If it's not a problem with your mom, I would be honored to be there. During our down times, everybody in the unit would talk about their families at home. I feel like your dad introduced me to you and your mom long before I ever met you. I know he wanted me and the rest of the unit to keep an eye on you as you grew up."

"I can't tell you how much this means to me." Emotion breaks my voice.

"It's okay, I understand. By the way, ever since my wife saw the invitation, she's been bugging me to tell you she would make the cake for your party. I just need to know what flavor you want it to be."

"Wow! Are you sure? Heather's cakes are famous."

"Well, my wife is a consummate matchmaker. She's been rooting for the two of you for years now. It makes her incredibly happy to see you guys getting married."

"I don't even know what to say — other than thank you so much from the both of us. Holly will be beside herself. She was afraid we'd have to serve homemade cupcakes from a box. Holly has a thing for white cake with lemon filling."

"It's our pleasure. We'll see you at the wedding."

"All I have to do now is find a justice of the peace," I comment half under my breath.

"Funny you should mention that. I know someone with lots of practice marrying people. Let me call him and see if he's available."

"Thank you so much. A lot of people aren't thrilled Holly and I are getting married so soon. But I know it's the right thing to do."

"I'm not worried. I know where you came from and if you're anything like your dad, you've got this handled in a heartbeat."

CHAPTER EIGHT

HOLLY

I NEVER KNEW MY sister was such a stickler for fashion. She's been dragging me from mall to mall to find the exact pair of shoes to match my dress. It doesn't seem to matter to her that I'm just getting married at the justice of the peace. It's not like it will be televised on TV or anything.

"Sage, do we have to do this? Can't I get married in my bare feet or something?"

"Well … yeah if we lived in Florida, but we live in Oregon and it will be cold outside. Stop being a baby."

"I simply don't care about it as much as you do. You know that Nate has seen me near death in the hospital and he still loves me. I don't understand why I have to get all gussied up."

"Pictures, that's why. You don't want your kids to be completely mortified by what you looked like on your wedding day."

"Kids? We haven't even thought that far ahead. My husband-to-be is going off to war, so it's not like he will be around a bunch to make those kids even if the doctors decide it's okay for me to have them."

"Is Nate okay with you guys not having kids? He's really big on family legacy," my sister comments.

"I assume he is. We've talked about my CF, and he doesn't seem to be bothered. You know Nate, he always finds a way around everything."

"Did you talk to him more than once or did you just mention it in passing? Because I know my husband doesn't listen worth beans. It probably went over his head or something."

"Sage! Are you calling my fiancé stupid?"

"Guys don't pay attention to the fine details until it's too late."

"Well, I doubt that's the case with us. We have talked about this stuff ad nauseam. Just ask Nate, he'll tell you how much time I spent trying to give him all the reasons why he shouldn't marry me. Nate analyzes everything to death. He knows the risks. He's known them since we were in elementary school."

Sage ruffles my hair like she used to when we were kids. "I suppose you're right. I have a hard time believing you are old enough to get married. Still, I really couldn't choose anybody better for you even if I had ordered him up from a catalog."

"They don't get much better than Nathaniel Abernathy. He's been with me through thick and thin."

"Well, let's go reward the man for his good taste and get you some goodies for your honeymoon." My sister wags her eyebrows at me in a suggestive manner.

I choke back a laugh. If she only knew Nate and I

have been making love since my sixteenth birthday.

"We should stop in and see the good people at Suzanne's Foundations & Frills to see what they have for you," my sister suggests.

"Can we not and say we did? You know I like to sleep in sweats — with my socks on."

"You can dress like that any other night, but on your wedding night, you need to look like a beautiful package ready to be unwrapped."

"I have news for you big Sis," I say with a grin. "Nathan already looks at me that way. I don't have to dress up in all sorts of foo-foo to convince him I'm beautiful."

"Oh, I know. I've seen the way he watches you. Sometimes it seems like you're a juicy T-bone steak in his mind. He doesn't hide his intentions very well. He never did. Even when you guys were in junior high school, I figured that this day would come sooner or later. I just thought it would be later."

I grin at my sister. "Truth be told, me too. I figured we'd both be out of college and in our first jobs before we took this leap. It's funny how life works out far differently than you ever expect."

"Isn't it going to be hard on you to have him gone? The man takes exceptionally good care of you. Last year, he rushed you to the hospital two out of the three times you had to go. Who's going to take you once he's gone?"

"I don't know. I'll figure it out. He won't be gone forever. He'll only be gone for basic training and AIT and then I can join him."

"Oh my gosh, I didn't even think about the prospect of you moving. Are you sure you're up to that? You never know about some of the places where you might have to live. They might have terrible air quality or be up at an elevation where you can't breathe very well with your CF."

"Remember I told you Nate and I have had endless discussions about the impact of my cystic fibrosis on our lives together? That's one thing we talked about. We don't know what the future will hold, but Nate knows what I need and he'll do his darnedest to make sure I have it."

"What about college?" My sister's wearing a skeptical expression.

"I should be able to graduate in three terms with all those AP classes I took. By the time Nate's done with basic training and AIT, I should be almost finished. I'll wait until he gets stationed somewhere and join him."

"Wow, you are so much braver than I am," my sister remarks tearfully.

"I'm not brave. I'm simply in love with a man who has a mission in life beyond a nine-to-five job. I'll do what I have to do to support him. I'll miss all of you, but my place is with him. He has done everything he could do to make my life better for all these years. It's my turn to return the favor."

"You really have grown up. You will make a phenomenal wife," Sage gushes as she hugs me.

"I hope so, after all, I had you and Mom as role models. How could I go wrong?"

CHAPTER NINE

NATE

SITTING ACROSS FROM JUSTICE Gardner, I look around the ballroom at the hotel wondering how our little trip to the justice of the peace evolved into this.

"You look a little lost, son," Judge Gardner observes as he lays a reassuring hand on my shoulder. "Is everything okay?"

"I'm fine. I'm just a little overwhelmed. This was supposed to be an intimate ceremony with Holly and me. Somehow our small, modest plans turned into a regular wedding ceremony."

"It sometimes happens with our gang."

"Where did the flowers come from? Flowers weren't in our budget," I remark absently.

"It looks like Tyler Colton has struck again. That man is a true romantic. It looks like he enlisted the help of the Girlfriend Posse."

"Girlfriend Posse?" I ask, feeling very confused.

"My goddaughter, Kiera, has two best friends — Tara and Heather. They started calling themselves the

Girlfriend Posse because they always have each other's back," the justice explains.

"Tyler insisted his wife make our wedding cake, but that doesn't explain the flowers."

"It does if you consider how exponentially the Girlfriend Posse has grown over the years. I would venture to guess the flowers are from Gwendolyn who is the wife of my best friend. She owns a florist shop."

"I don't know if we'll have money to pay everyone back," I admit, feeling my panic rising with every disclosure. "That's why I planned to keep our wedding small."

Justice Gardner grins. "That's the beautiful thing about the Girlfriend Posse. You never have to pay back the help. It's just given for free because people care about you."

"I'm warning you; Holly will burst out into tears when she sees all these flowers."

"I haven't met many women who don't cry when they see flowers. I enjoyed meeting Holly — she is a spitfire, for sure."

"I can't argue with you. It's one of the things I love most about her."

"You know, it's a challenge to be married to a gal like that. My Isobel is quite a firecracker too. But, when it came down to it, it helped her battle cancer. So I am grateful for her moxie and fight."

"I know what you mean. Holly's attitude has a lot to do with how well she does with her cystic fibrosis. She is quite a fighter. If I had to struggle with all the things she does on a daily basis, I think I would be curled up in a catatonic ball somewhere."

"Usually, I don't say much to discourage a couple from getting married, but I need to ask you if you are prepared to lose her?"

I look down and trace the design on the carpet with the toe of my dress shoe as I formulate an answer. "I don't know if I will ever be prepared for that day; I'm not sure it's possible to be. If you're asking me if I know what's likely to happen, I do. However, I have hope a treatment is right around the corner."

"What if it's not?" Justice Gardner presses.

"Then I'll love her every day I can and be crushed when she's gone."

"I want you to understand the ramifications of what you're doing today."

"I've been falling deeper in love with Holly every day since the first day she yelled at me for taking her ball on the playground. Whether I'm married to her or not, I will love her until the day I die. It's not a choice for me. It just is. She is the oxygen I breathe."

"I have a daughter who is a paraplegic. Taking care of someone who is disabled is difficult, painful work."

"I am aware of that too, Your Honor. But it doesn't change my love for Holly."

Justice Gardner grins slowly and sticks his hand out for me to shake. "That's the answer I was looking for. Best of luck today and for the rest of your life. Now let's go get you married."

⸺⬤⬤⸺

I swallow hard as I try not to fiddle with my necktie. The reality of all this is closing in on me. Even though it's something I want to do, it still seems overwhelming. If you had asked me growing up whether I would be married before I turned twenty-one, I would have thought you were crazy. Holly and I met when we were so young and our relationship changed from adversaries to friends to lovers; there were no real hard and fast rules with us. We did what made sense to us at the time, and somehow, those choices brought us here.

Holly's brother, Ash, pokes me with his elbow. "You're not about to pass out over there, are you?"

His voice interrupts my trip down memory lane, and I jump. "No, that's not it at all. I was just thinking how far our relationship has come over the years. I'm excited to marry your sister."

"I'm tempted to give you the customary brother speech. I think I'll skip it, though. It's pretty obvious you love my sister and that you'll treat her right. I think you've probably had enough people question your decision. I'm not going to be one of them. I understand why you're willing to take the risk. I hope when I find my forever-after-woman she'll be as awesome as my big sister."

Ash and I have been friends for a long time because he's only a year younger than us. He is as fiercely protective of Holly as I am. To have his blessing means the world to me. I take a moment to collect myself. "Thanks for the endorsement. I hope you find someone like Holly too. I've never been this happy."

The door to the conference center opens, and Sage makes her way up the aisle. Although she looks beautiful, she is not who I am waiting for. Unconsciously, I hold my breath until I can catch a glimpse of Holly.

Tyler puts his hand on my shoulder and whispers, "I

know it's hard, but you need to breathe. If you don't, you'll be horizontal."

Taking a deep breath, I turn to him and smile as I mouth, "Thanks."

I should have been prepared for this moment. My mom has told me the story of how my dad dissolved into tears when he saw her coming up the aisle at their wedding so many times I've lost count. It's part of the romantic folklore which helps complete the image I have of my dad. I can't help but wonder if he would approve of my choice; something tells me he would.

I knew Holly would be beautiful. She always is — but today she is exquisite. Her long brown hair is artfully arranged in soft curls around her bare shoulders. Her lips curl up in a bemused smile as she sees tears form in the corner of my eyes.

"I love you," she whispers to me as she stands in front of me and holds my hands between us. "Welcome to the beginning of us as one."

Chapter Ten

Holly

As I listen to the monotonous sounds of my nebulizer as it threatens to drown out the dance music in the room next door, I can't help but grin like a fool.

When Nate and I discussed the idea of using a justice of the peace, I hid my disappointment. A day like today was just a pipe dream for me. I never thought it would happen in real life. Sure, Nate and I had talked about getting married since he gave me a promise ring at fifteen. Still, I figured at some point he would change his mind. How miraculous is it that he never wavered? I know for certain I am one of the luckiest women on the planet.

Our thrown-together wedding ended up being one of the most romantic weddings I've ever seen. I have no idea how Nate pulled it off.

Nate comes into the little office carrying a plate of food and a glass of punch.

"Mrs. Abernathy, your dinner is served."

I turn off the nebulizer. "Oh my gosh, that's the first time anyone has said my name out loud. It's really real, isn't it?"

"Yeah, we are official. Judge Gardner has already signed everything."

"I know, I thought my dad was going to dissolve into a puddle of tears when he signed as a witness."

"My mom wasn't far behind," Nate acknowledges.

"Your mom was amazing today when she helped me get ready. I think she is finally on board with the whole wedding thing."

"She has changed her tune since she talked to the recruiter. I guess I might be stateside more often than I initially thought."

I frown as I say, "That little development is because of me, right?"

"In all honesty, it probably was. I wasn't planning to say anything about your cystic fibrosis. I didn't figure it was any of the Army's business — or at least not until we have to change doctors."

"So what changed?"

"When my mom talked to the recruiter, she decided to brag about how brave you were."

I sigh. "I wish people didn't think I was so brave and inspirational. I just want to live my life like a regular person."

"I know. My mom didn't mean any harm. I think she thought she was building me up in the eyes of the recruiter."

"Does it mean you may not be able to go and help fight the insurgents?"

"I don't know for sure — but it probably means

they'll use me to teach other people Arabic. My recruiter talked about waiting to enlist until I graduate from college. It turns out that the combination of my education degree together with my focus in languages would make me a great candidate for officer candidate school. However, I need to have a degree before I pursue OCS."

"Are you okay with waiting?" I search his face for clues about how he really feels about this development.

Nate shrugs. "I can't deny that I would like a chance to serve in the same spot as my dad. However, I have other considerations now. If I teach other people to speak Arabic, my influence can be multiplied, don't you think?"

"Yes, I do. You're a natural born teacher; you'd do so well teaching classes."

"That's what I thought. The more I thought about it, the more it makes sense. It's like having the best of both worlds; I get to serve my country, but I get to stay near you too."

"So, you don't feel like you're settling for something you don't want to do? I would hate that. I don't want to be the person who holds you back. I want to be the person who puts the wind in your sails."

"I think this falls under everything happens for a reason," I remark as I roll my shoulder. "The new plan is probably far better than the plan I came up with for myself. It'll make my mom happy because I will graduate from college with my scholarship and it will make me happy because I get to stay with my new wife for a while."

"Will you still have to go away to basic training and AIT?"

I shrug. "I don't know all of those details precisely yet. I understand the training is similar. I would just go through with other officers."

"Then I think it's a good thing your mom spilled the beans about me."

"I guess." Nate shrugs. "My whole life I've cringed every time she over shared, but this time it actually helps us."

"Who knew there was a perk to having cystic fibrosis? If it helps keep you alive, I don't resent it so much."

"You might change your mind if I start to get middle-age spread from having a desk job," Nate jokes.

"I'll just have to be a nagging wife and make sure you work out regularly."

"I'm gonna hold you to that," Nate answers with a smile.

"Speaking of exercise, I am finished with my breathing treatment, so I am good to go. I want to dance with my new husband."

"That sounds like a spectacular idea. From the sound of things, the party is in full swing. Tyler is having a good time entertaining people with his guitar. I never even knew he played, but it's pretty awesome."

"Let's go! I can't wait to see the cake from Heather. I have no idea what it looks like. She just asked me a bunch of questions about what we like and told me it was a surprise."

"I haven't seen it either, they sent me out of the room before they brought it in."

Nate places his arm around my waist and draws me

close. "I hope you don't mind if I kiss my wife. The last kiss was a little too public for my liking."

"By all means, I think you signed up for a lifetime of kissing me," I answer.

Nate tightens his embrace and kisses me with exquisite thoroughness.

Suddenly we are interrupted by a discreet cough. I spin around, embarrassed to have been caught.

"Don't feel like you have to stop on my account," Judge Gardner quips with a wink. "I came to tell you that your guests are getting a little restless. They want you to cut the cake."

I blush all the way to the roots of my hair as I answer, "We were headed that way, we just got a little distracted."

"Trust me, I've been married a long time. Distractions are good. Take your time. I'll simply have Tyler play another song."

"No, that's all right, I'll have other opportunities to kiss my wife," Nate answers as he walks me to the door.

When the double doors open, my brother announces, "Let's hear it for Mr. and Mrs. Abernathy!"

The whole room erupts in applause.

Nate bows slightly. "I did good, didn't I?"

My new mother-in-law responds in a clear voice, "Yes you did, son. Your dad would be so proud of you."

"I'm pretty proud of you too," I whisper.

"Okay, stop being such lovebirds and go cut the cake," my sister says.

Sage grabs my hand and drags me over to the cake table. "Close your eyes until I tell you to open them. I can't wait for you to see this. It's the best freakin' cake I've ever seen."

"I believe you," I squeak as she almost pulls me out of my shoes.

She guides me to a specific spot and instructs, "Okay, open your eyes!"

Nate must've been playing along too because we both exclaim in unison, "Wow!"

"It's perfect!" Nate says as he examines the cake.

"Heather, how did you know this is what I wanted?" I ask.

"I help a lot of brides and grooms, but I don't usually run across a love story quite as enduring as yours. I just thought you might want to see it in pictures."

I slowly walk around the cake, taking care not to trip on my train. It's our whole life in pictures spiraling up from the bottom. It starts with baby pictures and ends with the picture someone snapped at the restaurant when we got engaged. Everything is there from our awkward first dance to the prom and graduation.

"It's too pretty to eat," I say, as my voice breaks with emotion.

Heather laughs. "I hear that all the time, but cakes are meant to be eaten."

"I don't want to destroy the pictures. They perfectly capture how long we've been in love," I protest.

"I figured you might think that, so I have a slide presentation for you with all the pictures. You'll be able to keep your cake forever in digital format."

"Thank you so much. I don't even have words —" I respond tearfully.

"It was my pleasure. I love seeing people in love," Heather responds as she hugs me. She whispers in my ear, "One military spouse to the other, if you ever need anything, just call me."

"I will. I definitely will," I answer softly.

CHAPTER ELEVEN

NATE

WE KNEW WHEN WE got married that we would have to wait a few weeks until we had a break in school before we got to have a honeymoon. Our parents got together and splurged for a bed-and-breakfast on the coast and it's beautiful. It should all be perfect, but something is wrong. Very wrong — as in I'm about to blow my top wrong.

My beautiful bride is currently under a pile of blankets. Her teeth are chattering, and she coughs so hard she throws up.

"Stop looking at me like that," Holly declares hotly. "You're making me feel like I'm going to die right in front of you. I'm fine!"

"Holly, you are not fine. I've known you for almost ten years. I can tell when you're fine and when you're bluffing. You are so bluffing. You need to go to the hospital. You have a fever, and your lungs are not clearing even after you get a treatment."

"But we're on our honeymoon!" she protests weakly as a new round of coughing invades her body.

"We are. But your health comes before any fancy vacation. We will have other opportunities to celebrate our marriage, but you have to take care of yourself."

"You don't understand! My CF rules my life. I just have to work around it. I want this to be a special time — just between us. It's like the CF is some random hitchhiker trying to interject himself into our lives."

"I'm sorry, Hol. I wish I could wave a magic wand and have it all go away, but I can't."

"I just wanted a few days where I could forget it all."

"I know — but it can't be today. Today, you need to let me take you to the hospital. You are sick enough it's scaring me."

"Maybe if I use my nebulizer and inhalers more often, I can power my way through this," Holly pleads.

"No. I'm sorry but you can't, baby. You are burning up with fever. If we wait much longer, you are going to end up in the hospital for months."

"I bet you're sorry you ever agreed to marry me."

"That's not true. This is part of what I signed up for. I may hate what the CF does to you, but I love you."

Holly coughs violently. By the time she's done, she is trembling from head to toe.

"Nate?" she whispers, "Promise me we'll come back."

"You got it." I scoop her up and carry her out to my truck.

⬤

This is the longest drive known to mankind. I will the traffic in front of me to move faster—but on the narrow roads from the coast to Portland, it's just not happening.

They were so concerned about Holly's O2 sat, they didn't think twice before bundling her up on life-flight to hustle her off to Oregon Health Sciences University, the largest hospital in our area. Apparently, because it's a teaching hospital, they are more familiar with Holly's limitations than the small regional coastal hospital.

I've said goodbye to Holly a million times during our relationship, but I don't think I've ever faced one as scary as that. The doctors gave her some medication to help quiet her cough and an industrial load of antibiotics. As I suspected, she has a rip-roaring case of pneumonia. It was very sobering when the ER doctor put up her lung x-rays. It was a wall of white. I've been to the doctor with her enough to know that they should not be white. They should be dark.

The medical staff gave us a few moments to say goodbye before the helicopter took off. Holly looked so terrified, and there was nothing I could do. I've never felt so helpless in my life.

By the time the helicopter took off, she was almost asleep. It broke my heart to hear her whisper, "I'm sorry. I didn't mean for it to go this way."

I tried to be upbeat and cheerful as I said, "That's all right. You're Mrs. Abernathy now. We have plenty of time to do our honeymoon 'Take II.'"

"I hope so," she responded so quietly I had to lean down to hear her. "If I don't make it, please know you are the only person I ever loved."

"Holly, you'll pull through this. It'll be just like the other times," I insisted as I wiped away tears.

"I hope so Nate. I do. But I just don't know."

As I pound on my steering wheel in frustration as traffic slows to a crawl again, those words echo in my mind like an evil mantra.

I know I shouldn't think this way, but it's been a long time since I've seen her this weak. What if I don't make it in time? What if something happens on the helicopter and I'm not there?

⸺◆⸺

After I coax my woefully overheated truck up the steep, winding road to OHSU, I haphazardly park in front of the ER and run inside. I'm so disheveled and distressed that initially, the staff mistakes me for a new patient. I quickly explain who I am and why I'm there.

I wait for what seems like forever but is probably less than ten minutes before a nurse comes out to get me.

"How is she? How is my wife?" I demand as I follow the nurse down the hall to the ICU.

"We just got her settled in here. She's sleeping now. The trip took a lot out of her."

"Will she be okay?"

"You probably know that your wife's health is quite fragile. There is only so much we can do when there is an underlying disease."

"Can you translate that into layman's terms for me?"

"All I can tell you is at the moment she is resting comfortably." The nurse consults Holly's chart. "Her temperature is down a bit. However, her lungs are quite congested and her white blood cell count is elevated. It will be a long fight, but we'll do what we can."

"What can I do?" I ask desperately. "I'm not ready to

let her go."

"There's not much you can do except wait for the medication to kick in. It simply takes time. It will be a rough recovery. She'll need every bit of your positive energy."

"I'll do whatever I need to do," I answer. "You know how they say married couples are two halves of a whole? That's really true of us. I can't imagine life without her."

"Then don't. Be there for her, love her through it, and be patient."

"Patience is not my strong suit," I admit.

"Well, you'll have to learn. This probably isn't the first crisis Holly has faced and it won't be the last," the nurse advises with a grim smile.

CHAPTER TWELVE

HOLLY

"Nathaniel Abernathy, I love you, I do. But you have to stop hovering over me. You're driving me nuts." I gather my hair up and tie it in a knot to keep it out of my face. "I need to get this paper done for my Comparative Writing class. If I don't, I won't graduate."

"So sue me for being worried about you. You are working way too hard. You haven't taken a break in like four hours." He hands me a bottle of water.

"That's because I'm trying to concentrate. This stuff is hard. The footnotes are a pain. I have to keep my focus on what I'm doing or I'll mess them up."

"You promised you would take care of yourself. What will do you when I'm away at Officer Candidate School?"

"Gee, I don't know, 'Dad'."

Nate rakes his hand through his short-cropped hair. "Look, I'm just concerned. It's been less than a year since you almost died from pneumonia. I've never been so scared in my life."

"I know. Life with me is like a crazy roller coaster ride. Sometimes I'm up, and sometimes I'm down. Right now, things are good. My blood tests look normal, my lung capacity has increased, and the torn muscles in my rib cage are better. I'm on the mend."

"Okay, I'll concede you're doing better now, but if you keep stressing yourself out over school and not eating and drinking properly, you won't be okay in the long haul. I'm leaving soon and I won't be back for months. I'm terrified that it'll all happen again and I won't be here for you."

I sigh as I respond, "You're right, I need to be more careful and pace myself. However, even if I do, chances are eventually there will be a reoccurrence. That's just the way it is. My immune system's compromised and I have all sorts of nasty bacteria in my lungs. It'll flare regardless of what I do. I can only hope it happens when you're around."

"What will you do if it happens when I'm not here?" Nate presses.

I can't help myself. I look at him with utter disbelief and barely resist the urge to roll my eyes. "We've been friends for a decade. I know you know my parents and my siblings. If you're not here, they'll step up. I haven't even mentioned the whole circle of friends you introduced me to through Tyler Colton. You know if I say one peep, they will be all over themselves to help me."

Nate comes over and kisses the side of my neck. "I'm sorry if I sound like a complete worrywart. I'm just frustrated we can't be together while I'm at training. Do you realize it'll be the first time we've been apart for more than a couple weeks since we were eleven?"

I arch into his kiss. "I understand. I'm scared too, but I'm also tough. We'll get through this, I promise. You can't get rid of me that easily — you married me for better or for worse. Sometimes it's better and sometimes it's worse."

Nate picks me up from my office chair and carries me over to the bed with ease. "I know that in my head. Convincing my heart you'll be okay while I'm gone is a little harder." I smile up at him. He is such a big teddy bear of a man. He tries to be all tough, but his heart is tender.

"I swear I will do everything in my power to keep the CF at bay. I want you to be able to focus on passing your training with flying colors. If I get into trouble, I will call someone. I know I was too stubborn during our honeymoon and it cost me. I won't make that mistake again."

"I want you to graduate, but I don't want you to wear yourself out doing it. Please be careful."

"Okay. I'll start with tonight. Since my concentration has been blown to pieces, I'll just have to do something else. Do you have any suggestions?" I try my best to smile seductively.

"Why Mrs. Abernathy, are you propositioning me?" Nate asks before he kisses me.

"I think I am, Mr. Abernathy. It is my prerogative to do so as your wife."

"That is a spectacular plan." Nate grins. "It sounds a lot more fun than Comparative Literature."

"I can't argue with you." I smirk. "Although eventually I'll have to get back to my school work. But, for now, I welcome the distraction."

When I look around Joy and Tiers, I can't hide my shock. I knew Heather was well known and talented, but I had no idea how famous she was. In the window of her shop is a showpiece I saw on a documentary about cake decorating. I still can't believe she made a cake for my tiny wedding.

Heather comes out of the back room carrying a tray of pastries. When she sees me, she puts down the pastries and runs over to give me an enormous hug.

"I can't believe you're here. I'm quite far from where you live. I remember the distance well. I made that trip with a stacked wedding cake."

"I know, but it was worth it just to see your shop." I can't hide the awe in my voice. "I feel silly now."

"Why do you feel silly?" Heather asks with a quizzical look.

"Well, I came to ask if I could book you for an anniversary cake. But I guess I never realized that you probably make cakes for movie stars and rich people."

"Don't be silly. I make cake for everyone. If you don't believe me, just ask my friends. They get sick of my cake. I'm no longer impressive to them. It's nice to have a new fan."

"Are you sure? I don't have a very large budget."

"Don't worry about it. We'll work something out. After all, you're a military wife now. We take care of our own."

"Actually, that's why I'm here. We need to celebrate our anniversary early. Nate and I are getting ready to graduate from college, and he already has a date to go to training. It's a few weeks before our first anniversary, so, I thought maybe it would be cool to have a party to celebrate our anniversary and the start of his new career."

"That sounds like a phenomenal idea. What do you think you would like to do as a theme?"

I blush as I respond, "Umm … I had to be a little underhanded to pull this off." I hand her a thumb drive.

"You wouldn't believe the things I have found on thumb drives," Heather says skeptically. "What am I looking for?"

"I got him to try on his cap and gown and a suit that is very near what dress greens will look like. I snuck a few pictures of us using the voice activation feature of my phone."

"Clever." Heather gives me a wink. "Maybe the wrong person is joining the military. So … what am I doing with these pictures?"

"I would like you to make a small cake like our wedding cake and just continue the journey using our wedding pictures, graduation pictures, and the one that looks like a military uniform."

"That's an amazing idea! I'm down with that."

"Great! Nate is having a hard time seeing the future right now. He seems stuck in the past. All he can see is the specter of me in the ICU. It's frustrating because there's more to me than my illness."

"Let me guess; he's clinging to you tighter than Saran Wrap and treating you like you can't even tie your own shoes, right?"

"Oh my Gosh! Yes. That's exactly what it's like. He seems to have forgotten I'm a fully capable adult and can function on my own."

"It's not you. I think it happens to everybody. When

you are married to someone with a natural need to be a hero, it's hard for them to understand that they don't always have to be the hero."

"So, what should I do about all of this? He's watched me do a decade worth of homework; it hasn't killed me yet," I shrug.

"In my experience, they have to work out their ghosts on their own. Trust me, after he's gone for a few days, you'll miss his grumpy, overprotective self."

"I know — that's what I'm afraid of. Nate has been by my side for half my life. I don't know what I'm going to do without him."

"I won't lie to you and say it's easy, because some days it's really hard. There is a whole community of people out there to give you moral support and hugs if you need them."

"I plan to take you up on that. Thank you so much for being there."

"Try not to worry about it too much. In the meantime, we have a party to plan. It might be time to call in the Girlfriend Posse."

"I've heard stories about your ability to throw parties and I'm more than a little nervous."

"Don't sweat it! We've got you covered," Heather says as she pulls out a legal pad to take notes.

EPILOGUE

NATE

WATCHING MY WIFE IS one of my favorite hobbies. I'll miss this probably more than anything else. She is beautiful when she sleeps, when she plays with the dog, or when she's concentrating on something she's reading. There isn't a time she doesn't capture my soul. I don't know how much I'll be able to contact her in a couple of weeks. Just to be safe, I upgraded our WebCam so I can see her when we speak.

Today is no exception. She looks radiant and healthy. There are no signs she is sliding backward again. But, there is something going on with her. I just can't figure out what. For lack of a better term, she's twitchy today.

In the middle of packing, I went into the bedroom to change my shoes and she about jumped out of her chair. Later, when I was coming in from loading the car, she was on the phone talking to someone and hung up abruptly. She's not usually like this. When I ask if everything is okay, she insists it is. Yet, I can't get over the feeling she's keeping something from me.

I glance over at her as she's sleeping in the car just to

make sure my impression of her today is not wrong. She's not flushed with fever or pale. However, as we head back over to our vacation villa on the coast to resume our honeymoon, I can't help but be worried she might be hiding something about her health. She's been working exceptionally hard to graduate — we both have. Finals week takes a toll on anyone's marriage.

Holly's temper has been short the last couple of weeks but, then again, so has mine. Maybe the fact that I'm leaving has become a little too real. It seemed so easy on paper, but put into practice, it's much harder. I know this career move will improve our lives in the long run, but at the moment, I'm more worried about the short-term impact.

My excitement over starting a new career is tempered by my fear of leaving my wife behind. I know it's only for a few months, but from this end of things, it seems like forever.

An ambulance comes barreling toward us in the oncoming lane with lights and sirens blaring. In a heartbeat, my mind goes back to the way Holly looked the last time we drove this road. Even this many months later, I feel the urge to throw up when I remember those long days in the ICU. Truth be told, a year ago I wasn't sure if my wife would pull through.

As I pull the car over to allow the ambulance to pass, Holly wakes up.

"What's going on? Is there an accident?" she says as she yawns.

"I'm not sure yet. I don't see anything. It's just the ambulance."

"Why do you look terrified?" Holly says with

concern in her voice.

"Don't worry about it. I just had an ugly flashback to the last time I dealt with this road, sirens, and paramedics. It's not my favorite memory on the planet."

"I know what you mean. I'm the same way. The sound of helicopter blades makes my heart race."

"Are you really feeling better? No sign of a relapse?" I probe.

"Nate, I promised you I would tell you if things were not right. They are fine. I am feeling strong and healthy. I won't make the same mistake I made before."

"I know. I trust you. I just … I mean … This road represents days and days of a living nightmare for me," I stammer.

"I'm sorry. I never meant to scare you. I just didn't want my stupid health issues to interrupt my honeymoon. I know it sounds stupid and vain. I wanted to ignore my awful illness. Honeymoons are supposed to be perfect and beautiful. I understand I made a horrible choice and I won't do it again."

"I think we both learned some really important lessons that day."

"Oh yeah? I learned I need to let you know how I'm feeling. What did you learn?"

"Something I thought I knew before, but that day brought it home to me in a way I never imagined. I need to cherish each and every moment with you because I might not have more — that's what I learned."

"I think your mom would agree, everyone needs to live that way. That's not something reserved for me because of my illness. It applies to everyone on the planet."

"That's true. My dad wasn't much older than me when he was killed. I know my mom never expected anything to happen. She thought Dad was in one of the safer units. After all, most of the people who needed Arabic translators were already checked for weapons and explosives before they ever talked to my dad. In a way, she was blindsided."

"I feel awful for Tracy. All these years later and she's still heartbroken. That's a long time to live with pain and be alone."

"I know. I've tried to talk her into dating, but she's just not interested. She says she married the one great love of her life and there will never be another person like my dad. As much as I love the romance of that, it hurts me to see my mom lonely."

"Well, I will do my best to spend time with her while you're gone. I don't want her to feel alone." Holly's phone vibrates against the seatbelt latch. She quickly picks it up and looks at it.

"Who's that?" I ask. "I bet it's my mom, I forgot to tell her we were leaving today."

"No, it's not your mom. A couple days ago, I mentioned to your mom that we were going back to our honeymoon villa. I got some good-natured teasing and an offer to go lingerie shopping. I was a little stunned. I turned her down, though. Who wants to go lingerie shopping with their mother-in-law? It'd be too weird."

"So, are you telling me you went lingerie shopping?" I ask with rapt attention as I pull my car into the parking area of the Bed and Breakfast.

Holly chuckles mysteriously. "I guess you'll have to

wait to find out."

"Ah man! You know I hate surprises."

"Consider it payback for our engagement dinner." She winks.

"*Touché*. I guess I deserve that." I stretch my back out as I get out of the car. "I can't wait to hop into the hot tub. Finals were brutal. I still have knots on top of my knots from all the stress."

"Poor baby," Holly murmurs when I open her door and help her out. "The hot tub sounds like a fabulous idea, but I want to go check out their new rec room. It sounds amazing."

Her request is odd, but this is Holly and sometimes what she finds interesting is a little offbeat. I shrug. "Okay, we'll stop by there before we get our keys."

"Oh, I forgot to tell you; Allison mailed us the keys because they're out of town until tomorrow. So, if the rec room is locked, we can still get in." Holly fishes a set of keys from her purse and hands them to me.

I slide my arm around her waist and we walk side-by-side to a building which wasn't here the last time we came.

"Wow, look at those skylights. I bet that's impressive when there's a storm."

"Allison was telling me all about the library she installed in the rec room. You know how I love books. I can't wait to see what she's got in there. She said I could feel free to read anything I wanted to. Allison said if I start reading a book and I don't finish it, I can just trade it for one of my own. I think it's an excellent idea for travelers."

"Far be it from me to stand between you and books.

I know I'll probably always come in second place if there is a contest."

"Don't be silly. You are always first in my book," Holly says as she turns to kiss me.

Walking up to the door, I try the lock. "It looks like I'll have to use the key. I hope it fits. I don't want you to be disappointed if you don't have books on our honeymoon," I tease.

I unlock the door and feel around for the light switch.

As soon as I flip it, We're greeted with a chorus of "Happy Anniversary!"

Stunned, I blink my eyes to make sure I see what I think I'm seeing. Everybody who was at our wedding is in this room — even Judge Gardner.

I turn to Holly, "I'm not sure what's going on here, but at least I know why you were being cagey today. I was wondering if there was something wrong with you and you didn't want to tell me."

"Nate, I wouldn't do that to you. Come here — I want to show you something."

She walks me over to a table where Tyler and Heather are standing with wide smiles on their faces.

"What's this — a re-creation of our wedding cake?"

"Look closer," Holly instructs.

I study the cake for a moment. "That's not our past, it's our future. How in the world did you get graduation pictures and pictures of me in a military uniform?"

"I'll never tell my secrets, Second Lieutenant-to-be. I gathered all of our friends and family here so I could show you how proud I am to be a soldier's wife. I know there will be times that we will be separated and it will seem like an eternity — but, that's the price of freedom."

"So it is. But I'm glad I'm on the journey with you. I love you, Holly. I'll miss you every day I'm gone, but the time will go more quickly because I know you will be at home waiting for me."

"That's the plan. You once called me a supreme pest. Do you remember what I told you all those years ago?"

I grin as I respond, "I sure do. You told me you plan to be with me until infinity times infinity."

"As far as I'm concerned, nothing has changed."

As I lean down to kiss my wife, I hear Sage mumble. "Darn it, you two got me again. I should know I need to wear waterproof mascara."

THE END

The Hidden Beauty Series continues with Paths Not Taken.

Dear Reader,

Thanks for reading my novella. If you liked reading about people who are not so stereotypical, then I've got good news…

…there's more.

The next book in the series Paths Not Taken is about making choices not everyone understands.

It's bad enough when Jordan makes a fool out of herself at work. It's worse when she does it in front of a customer.

To make matters worse, after she walked away from her job, Jordan Shepherd has to go home and face her friends and family.

Jordan is not even sure anyone will want her around after what happened the last time she was around her brother, Jaxson.

While she's busy trying to figure out creative ways to eat crow. The customer who witnessed her last day at work wants to hire her to design clothes.

It's what she's always wanted to do. Is Jordan brave enough to throw caution to the wind and follow a new path?

If you like to root for unlikely heroes, this is the book for you.

Get Paths Not Taken now!

Get it now.

~Mary

Because love matters, differences don't.

ACKNOWLEDGEMENTS

I have known and loved many fine soldiers in my life both past and present. Thank you for being the inspiration for this book. The choices are never easy. The sacrifices you made do not go unnoticed.

ABOUT THE AUTHOR

I have been lucky enough to live my own version of a romance novel. I married the guy who kissed me at summer camp. He told me on the night we met that he was going to marry me and be the father of my children.

Eventually, I stopped giggling when he said it, and we've been married for over thirty years. We have two children. The oldest is a Doctor of Osteopathy. He is across the United States completing his residency, but when he's done, he is going to come back to Oregon and practice Family Medicine. Our youngest son is now tackling high school, where he is an honor student. He is interested in becoming an EMT.

I write full time now. I have published more than thirty books and have several more underway. I volunteer my time to a variety of causes. I have worked as a Civil Rights Attorney and diversity advocate. I spent several years working for various social service agencies before becoming an attorney.

In my spare time, I love to cook, decorate cakes and, of course, I obsessively, compulsively read.

I would be honored if you would take a few moments out of your busy day to check out my website, MaryCrawfordAuthor.com. While you're there, you can sign up for my newsletter and get a free book. I will be announcing my upcoming books and giving sneak peeks as well as sponsoring giveaways and giving you information about other interesting events.

If you have questions or comments, please E-mail me at Mary@MaryCrawfordAuthor.com or find me on the following social networks:

Facebook: www.facebook.com/authormarycrawford

Website: MaryCrawfordAuthor.com

Twitter: www.twitter.com/MaryCrawfordAut